Simon Abel

Poky Little Puppy's
Special Day

By Cindy West
Illustrated by Keenan Jones

A GOLDEN BOOK • NEW YORK
Western Publishing Company, Inc., Racine, Wisconsin 53404

There is a magical place called Little Golden Book Land, filled with wonderful things to see and do. Every day is a special day, just waiting to be discovered.

Poky Little Puppy was very excited. In just one week the Little Golden Book Land Games would begin. Everybody was getting ready for the swimming and jumping and running contests.

"I'm leading the opening parade," Poky Little Puppy told his friend Shy Little Kitten. "And I want to run in the relay race, too."

But when it came time to choose the teams for the relay race, nobody picked Poky Little Puppy. "Please give me a chance," he said.

"No, no," everyone replied. "You're much too slow."

Finally Saggy Baggy Elephant said, "You can be an alternate."

"What does that mean?" asked Poky Little Puppy.

"That means if someone can't race, you can take their place."

"Thank you!" said Poky Little Puppy. "I'm going to start practicing right away."

First Poky Little Puppy did some warming up.

He took a
deep breath,

he wiggled
his ears,

he wagged
his tail,

and he waved his
little legs in the air.

"Now I'm ready to run!" said Poky Little Puppy. Huffing and puffing, he raced up the hill. "Whew!" he panted as he passed Saggy Baggy Elephant dancing his favorite one-two-three-kick.

"Running is such hard work," Poky Little Puppy called as he ran by. "But I have to be in good shape if I'm going to be an alternate in the relay race."

"Right," said Saggy Baggy Elephant. "I'll have to remember to do a little running myself, after I'm through dancing."

Poky Little Puppy trotted by the stream and waved to Scuffy the tugboat. Scuffy blew his whistle and chugged along beside him.

"Hey, Poky. You're doing great," Scuffy called out.

"Thanks," Poky Little Puppy replied as he picked up speed.

Then Poky Little Puppy ran by Baby Brown Bear, who was snacking on a big bowl of honey.

"Aren't you going to practice for the race?" asked Poky Little Puppy, panting.

"Nope. I'm such a fast runner, I don't have to practice."

"Well, I *do*," gasped Poky Little Puppy as he ran on.

Finally the Little Golden Book Land Games
began! Tootle and Katy Caboose joyfully carried
trainloads of lions, elephants, and rabbits down
from the Jolly Jungle.

Poky Little Puppy proudly led the parade down
Main Street. He carried the flag as the marching
bands played, "Oompah-pah! Oompah-pah!"

Then it was time for the relay race.

But a terrible thing happened near the starting line. Tawny Scrawny Lion tripped over his tail! "Ouch! Ouch!" he groaned.

"Oh, no!" said Poky Little Puppy. "Are you all right?"

"I've sprained my paw," said Tawny Scrawny Lion. "Poky, you're going to have to run in my place."

"I'm ready," said Poky Little Puppy. "I won't let you down."

"All right," said Saggy Baggy Elephant. "Keep your eyes on this baton. I'll begin the race and then pass it to Baby Brown Bear. After he runs, he will pass it to you. Then it'll be your turn to run!"

Tootle blew his whistle. "On your mark, get set, go!"
Saggy Baggy Elephant ran and thumped as fast as
he could, but he just wasn't fast enough. "I guess I
shouldn't have stayed up dancing so late last night,"
he thought as the lion from the other team whizzed
right by him.

"Here!" gasped Saggy Baggy Elephant, passing the baton to Baby Brown Bear. "I hope you can run faster than I did!"

Baby Brown Bear dragged his body up the hill. "I've been eating too much honey lately. I can't keep up with the elephant from the other team."

"It's up to you!" said Baby Brown Bear, panting, as he passed the baton to Poky Little Puppy. Poky snatched it and took off like the wind. He caught up with the rabbit from the other team in no time at all. The two were running neck and neck as they rounded the last turn toward the finish line.

FINISH

Then Poky Little Puppy put on a burst of speed and pulled ahead of the rabbit. He kept pushing himself and won the race by a nose!

"You did it!" cheered Tawny Scrawny Lion.
"You won the race for our team!"
Saggy Baggy elephant and Baby Brown Bear
covered him with hugs.

As Poky Little Puppy was awarded his blue
ribbon, he asked, "Whose team can I be on next
year?"

"Ours! Ours! Ours!" shouted everyone.

And Poky Little Puppy smiled and smiled.